Magic Kitten

A
Christmas
Surprise

Magic Kitten

A
Christmas
Surprise

SUE BENTLEY

Illustrated by Angela Swan

SCHOLASTIC INC.

To Tibby, my fondly remembered marmalade sweetie.

First published in Great Britain in 2007 by Penguin Books Ltd.

ISBN 978-0-545-82938-0

12 11   19/0

Printed in the U.S.A.   40

First Scholastic printing, December 2014

★ Prologue ★

Dust swirled around the young white lion's paws as he raced through the valley. Flame knew he shouldn't risk being out in the open. What if his uncle Ebony saw him?

Suddenly, Flame heard a terrifying roar as an enormous black adult lion burst out from behind some trees. The lion bounded toward Flame.

"Ebony," called Flame.

Flame leaped into the grass to hide. A bright white light flashed in the air and suddenly Flame had turned into a tiny, snowy-white kitten with a fluffy tail. The magic had worked again!

Flame's heart thudded in his tiny chest as he edged backward to where the grass grew thicker. His uncle Ebony was very close. Flame hoped this disguise would protect him, as it had so many times before.

Flame heard a rustle in the grass and a dark shape pushed toward him. Flame was ready to fight. His emerald eyes sparkled with anger and fear.

"Stay there, Prince Flame. I will protect you," growled a deep but gentle voice.

Flame meowed in relief as an old gray lion peered down at him.

"Cirrus. I am glad to see you again. I

had hoped that by now, Ebony would be ready to give back the throne he stole from me," Flame said.

Cirrus shook his head. "That will never happen. Your uncle is determined to rule in your place. He sends spies to search for you. It is not safe for you to be here. Use this disguise and go back to the other world to hide."

The tiny kitten bared his sharp teeth as he looked up into Cirrus's face. "I wish I could fight him now!" Flame cried.

Cirrus's eyes flickered with affection. He reached out a huge paw and gently pet Flame's tiny fluffy white head.

"You are brave, Prince Flame. But now is not the time. Come back when you are stronger," Cirrus said.

Suddenly, Cirrus and Flame heard another roar from nearby. The ground shook as huge paws pounded through the tall grass.

"You cannot hide from me, Flame!" roared Ebony.

"Save yourself, Prince Flame. Go quickly!" Cirrus said.

Sparks glowed in the tiny kitten's silky white fur. Flame meowed as he felt the magic building inside him. He felt himself falling . . . the magic was working.

Chapter
ONE

"I really hope it's going to be a white Christmas!" Molly Paget said, peering hopefully out of the window. She sighed as raindrops snaked down the glass and blurred her view of the street outside. "Oh, well. There's still a week to go."

Molly jumped down the stairs two at a time and went into the kitchen where a delicious spicy smell filled the air. Her mom was just taking a tray of muffins out of the oven.

Mrs. Paget looked up and smiled. "I heard you running down the stairs. What's the hurry?"

Molly grinned. "There isn't one. I'm just in a good mood. Can I have one of those muffins?"

Her mom nodded. "Of course you can. Take one of those on the plate, they're cooler."

Molly picked up a muffin and took a bite. "Mmm, yummy. Tastes Christmasy!"

Her mom smiled. "I'm glad it passes the Molly test!"

"When are Gran and Gramps arriving?" Molly asked, munching.

Her grandparents lived near the coast. She hadn't seen them since the summer, but they were going to spend Christmas at Molly's house. Molly's eyebrows dipped in a small frown as she remembered how during the last visit to her grandparents' house, she had had to take her shoes off before going into the living room. Everyone always sat at the table to eat and no one was allowed to watch TV during the day. Molly hoped Gran would be less strict this Christmas.

"They'll be here the day before Christmas Eve," her mom said, wiping her hands on her apron. "I've still got desserts to make, a cake to ice, and tons of presents to buy. And we haven't even started clearing out the spare bedroom." A worried look came over her face. "Your Gran's great, but she has very high standards."

Tell me about it, Molly thought. "I'll help you. I'm good at clearing up and stuff," she said brightly.

"It's nice of you to offer, but Molly

and the word *help* can sometimes spell trouble!" Mrs. Paget said wryly, ruffling her daughter's blond hair. "I'll get your dad to give me a hand with the bedroom. It's his parents who are staying, after all."

"Did I hear my name?" Mr. Paget said, coming into the kitchen. His hair was speckled with dust and there were cobwebs sticking to his blue sweater. He quickly washed his hands before helping himself to a muffin.

"Da-ad! You've got yucky stuff all over you," Molly said, laughing. She reached up to pick off a cobweb.

"Do I? I didn't notice," Mr. Paget said around a mouthful of muffin. "I was just in the attic. I had to move a mountain of old stuff to get to the Christmas tree and decorations. Anyway, I found them in the end. They're in the living room."

"Great!" Molly said excitedly, already speeding out of the kitchen. "I'm going to put the tree up right now!"

"Slow down, Molly!" her mom called after her.

But Molly had already left. Mr. Paget shook his head slowly. "Molly's only got two speeds. Fast and faster!" he said as he followed his daughter.

By the time her dad came into the living room, Molly had her arms full of folded, green spiky branches. "There's an awful lot of tree," she said, peering into the long box. "I don't remember it being so huge."

Mr. Paget laughed. "Well, it couldn't have grown since last year, could it, you silly? I'll get the stepladder."

"That's a job well done!" Mr. Paget said an hour later.

Molly looked up at the Christmas tree, which almost touched the living-room ceiling. "It's impressive. I can't wait to decorate it!" She searched in another cardboard box and found some tissue-wrapped packages. Unwrapping one of them, she looked closely at the blue glass ornament. "Isn't this pretty? It's got silver-frosted snowflake patterns all over it," she said delightedly. "Do we have any more like this?"

Her dad nodded. "There are lots of them. I remember them hanging on our Christmas tree when I was little."

"Really? They must be ancient then," Molly said.

Mr. Paget grinned, giving her a playful nudge in the arm. "I forgot we had those ornaments. Be very careful with them."

"I will," Molly promised, unpacking the precious ornaments very gently.

Mr. Paget peered into the empty cardboard box. "That's funny. I thought the tinsel and other stuff was in there, too. Maybe it's in the garage. I'll go and look."

Molly frowned. She knew that her dad couldn't resist cleaning when he was looking for things. He would take forever. "Aw, do you have to do it now, Dad?"

Mr. Paget grinned at the look on her face. "Impatient to get going, aren't you? Why don't you start on the bottom branches? But you'd better wait for me to come back before you do the higher ones."

"Okay!" Molly said, already tearing open a packet of little green plastic hooks.

As soon as he'd left, she began hanging ornaments on the tree. Soon, the bottom branches were finished. Molly stood back to admire the way

the blue, red, and gold glass gleamed prettily against the dark green.

Her dad still hadn't come back. Molly looked longingly up at the higher branches. She shifted her feet impatiently. "Come on, Dad, you slowpoke," she grumbled. She hesitated for a minute and then dragged the step-ladder closer to the tree.

He was bound to be back in a minute. She'd just start doing a few more branches. Climbing halfway up the ladder, she began hanging ornaments on the branches that were within easy reach.

This is easy, she thought. *I don't know what Dad was worrying about.*

She climbed higher to hang more

decorations. At this rate, she'd have the whole tree finished soon. At the top of the ladder, Molly leaned out farther to try and reach a branch near the top of the tree that would look perfect with the ornament she was holding.

And then she felt the ladder wobble.

"Oops!" Throwing out her arms, Molly tried to grab something to steady herself, but her fingers closed on thin air. She lost her balance and banged against the tree. It shook wildly and decorations began falling off in all directions.

Molly heard the precious ornaments smash into tiny pieces as they hit the carpet. "Oh, no!" she cried.

She looked down as she swayed

sideways, and then everything seemed to happen at once. The ladder and tree both tipped sideways and started to fall to the ground.

"He-elp!' Molly croaked, tensing her whole body for the painful bruising thud as she hit the carpet.

Suddenly, the room filled with a dazzling white flash and a shower of silver sparks. Molly felt a strange warm tingling sensation down her spine as she fell. The air whistled past her ears. There was a sudden jolt, but no hard landing.

To her complete shock, Molly was hovering in midair half a foot above the carpet. Swirling all around her was a snowstorm of brightly sparkling glitter!

She gasped as she felt herself turning
and then drifting gently down to the
carpet where she landed on her behind
with barely a bump. The sparkling
glitter fizzed like a firework and then
disappeared.

Molly sat up shakily and looked
around.

The ladder was upright and the tree was straight and tall once again. The delicate glass ornaments were all unbroken and hanging back in place on the branches.

But . . . I heard them smash! I don't get it . . . Molly said to herself. What had just happened? She felt like pinching herself to see if she was dreaming.

"I hope you are not hurt?" meowed a strange little voice.

Molly almost jumped out of her skin. "Who said that?" She twisted around, her eyes searching the room.

Crouching beneath the Christmas tree, Molly saw a tiny fluffy snow-white kitten. Its silky fur seemed to glitter with a thousand tiny, diamond-bright

sparkles and it had the biggest emerald
eyes she had ever seen.

Chapter
TWO

Molly's eyes widened. She must be more confused and shaken up by her fall than she'd thought. She'd just imagined that the kitten had spoken to her!

She looked at the kitten again and now its silky white fur and bushy tail looked normal. Perhaps it had wandered in when her dad left the door open on his way to the garage. "Hello. Where'd you come from?" she said, kneeling down and reaching a hand toward it.

"I come from far away," the kitten meowed. "When I saw you fall I used my magic to save you. I am sorry if I startled you."

Molly gasped and pulled her hand back as if she had been burned. "You . . . you can talk!" she stammered.

The kitten blinked up at her with wide green eyes. Despite its tiny size, it didn't seem to be too afraid of her. "Yes. My name is Prince Flame. What is yours?"

"Molly. Molly Paget," Molly said. Her mind was still whirling and she couldn't seem to take this all in. But she didn't want to scare this amazing kitten away, so she sat back on her heels and tried to stay as small as possible. "Um . . . I don't know how you did it, but thanks for helping me. I could have hurt myself badly."

"You are welcome," Flame purred, and his tiny kitten face took on a serious look. "Can you help me, Molly? I need somewhere to hide."

"Why do you need to do that?" Molly asked.

Flame's emerald eyes lit up with anger. "I am heir to the Lion Throne. My uncle Ebony has stolen it and rules in my place. He wants to keep my throne, so he sends his spies to find me."

"*Lion* Throne?" Molly said doubtfully, looking at the tiny kitten in front of her.

Flame didn't answer. He backed away from the Christmas tree and before Molly knew what was happening, she was blinded by another bright silver flash. For a moment she couldn't see anything. But when her sight cleared, the kitten had gone and in its place a magnificent young white lion stood proudly on the carpet.

Molly gasped, scrambling backward on her hands and knees. "Flame?"

"Yes, it is me, Molly," Flame replied in a deep velvety roar.

Molly gulped, just getting used to the great majestic lion, when there was a final flash of dazzling light and Flame reappeared as a silky white kitten.

"Wow! I believe you," she whispered. "That's a cool disguise. No one would ever know you're a prince!"

Flame pricked his tiny ears and started to tremble. "My uncle's spies will recognize me if they find me. Will you hide me, please?"

Molly reached out and pet Flame's soft little head. He was so tiny and helpless-looking. Her soft heart melted. "Of

course I will. You can live with me. It'll
be great having you to cheer me up if
Gran gets in one of her grumpy moods.
I bet you're hungry, aren't you? Let's go
and find you some food."

Flame gave an eager little meow.

"Find who some food?" said her dad, coming into the room with a big cardboard box in his arms.

Molly jumped up and turned to face him. "Dad! Something amazing just happened. I almost fell off the ladder . . . I mean . . . er . . ." she stopped guiltily, deciding that it might be smart to skip that part. "I've just found the most amazing kitten and I'm going to look after him. And guess what, he's magic and he can ta—" she stopped suddenly again as Flame gave a piercing howl.

"Flame? What's wrong?" Molly said, crouching down to talk to him.

Flame blinked at her and then sat down on the rug and began calmly washing himself in silence. Molly looked at him, puzzled. Why didn't he explain?

"You and your imagination, Molly Paget! A talking kitten?" Her dad shook his head slowly. "I don't know where that little kitten came from, but you should look outside and see if one of the neighbors is looking for him!"

"No, they won't be . . ." Molly started to say, but she saw Flame raise a tiny paw and put it to his mouth, warning her to keep quiet. "I'll go check on the neighbors," she finished quickly. She picked Flame up and went into the front garden. "What was all that about back there?" she asked him once they were alone.

"I did not have time to explain before your father came in that you cannot tell anyone my secret," Flame meowed softly. "You must promise, Molly."

"Oh, no!" Molly's hands flew to her mouth. "But I almost told Dad everything. Have I already put you in danger?"

Flame shook his head. "No, it is okay. He did not believe you. Luckily, grown-up humans seem to find it difficult to believe in magic."

Molly breathed a huge sigh of relief as she looked into Flame's serious little face. "I promise I'll keep your secret from now on. Cross my heart and hope to die."

Flame nodded, blinking at her happily.

"I guess we should go and pretend

to look for your owner. Come on," Molly urged.

"So we'll just have to keep Flame . . ." Molly finished explaining as she faced her mom half an hour later. Flame nestled in her arms, purring contentedly.

Mrs. Paget was putting things in the dishwasher. She stood up and reached out to pet Flame's soft little white ears. "Oh, dear, we hadn't planned on having a kitten, especially with your grandparents coming. But if you've asked all around . . ." she said uncertainly.

"Oh, I did. I went to *dozens* of houses and no one knew anything about a white kitten," Molly lied. "So—can I open a can of tuna for Flame?"

Her mom smiled. "Sure. He's really gorgeous, isn't he? And I like his name. But I think that you might have to keep Flame in your bedroom while your Gran's here."

Molly frowned. "Why? What does she have against kittens?"

Mrs. Paget smiled. "It's not just kittens, it's pets in general. She won't tolerate hair on the furniture. As for muddy paw prints, wet fur, fleas— should I go on?"

"Flame doesn't have fleas!" Molly exclaimed. "Anyway, once Gran meets him I bet even she's going to love him, too. He's the cutest kitten ever."

"I agree with you. But I wouldn't be too sure that your gran will," her mom

warned gently.

Molly hardly heard her. "Come on, Flame, let's go and tell Dad that Mom says you can stay." Flame looked up at her and gave an extra loud purr.

Chapter
THREE

"It's the last day of the semester, so we'll be just doing fun stuff at school instead of lessons," Molly said to Flame as she pulled on her coat a couple of days later.

Flame had followed her into the hall, his fluffy white paws padding on the carpet.

"I have to hurry and catch the bus now, so I'll see you later," Molly said, bending down to pet him. "I really love having you living here and I wish you

could come with me, but we aren't
allowed to bring pets to school."

"But I can come!" Flame told her
with a happy little meow. "I will use
my magic to make myself invisible.
Only you will be able to see and hear
me."

"Really? That's *so* cool!" Molly said happily. "Okay then. Quick, can you get into my backpack before Mom and Dad see you and say you can't come with me?"

Flame nodded and jumped inside.

It was a short bus ride to school. Molly put her bag on her lap, so Flame could poke out his head and look at the brightly decorated stores and the big Christmas tree in town. Fairy lights glinted in the trees lining the streets and more colored lights were strung outside the big stores.

Flame's green eyes grew round with wonder. "I have never seen so many bright lights. They are like glowworms in a field of grass," he meowed.

"It's because of Christmas," Molly explained in a whisper. "The shops are full of presents and stuff and special treats."

Flame put his head on one side. "What is Christmas?"

"Oh, I forgot. I guess you don't have that in your world, do you?" Molly said. "Christmas is a special time, when the family gets together to celebrate the baby Jesus being born. We sing carols and give each other presents and eat lots of delicious food until we feel like bursting." She grinned.

Flame looked a bit confused. "It sounds very strange, but I think I will like Christmas."

Molly smiled. She decided to buy

him a really special present and put it
under the tree for him to unwrap on
Christmas morning.

The bus stopped outside the school.
Molly got off and put her bag on her
shoulder as she walked toward the
school gate. A thin, pretty girl with long

blond hair came running up. It was Shona Lamb, one of the most popular girls in Molly's class.

"Hey, Molly!"

"Hi, Shona!" Molly replied. She noticed that Shona was wearing some fabulous new boots. "Wow! When did you get those?" she asked admiringly. The boots were like the ones Molly wanted for Christmas, only more expensive-looking.

Shona glanced down at her cool boots. "What? Oh, yesterday. I'd forgotten about them already. But listen, I am *so* excited! I bet you can't guess what Mom's going to buy me for Christmas!"

Molly pretended to think hard. "A

sports car, a trip around the world, your own private plane?" she joked.

"Very funny. You're a riot!" Shona said, rolling her eyes. "It's a pony! I'm starting riding lessons soon. You'll be able to come over and watch me ride my very own pony!"

"Um . . . yes," Molly murmured, imagining Shona prancing about and showing off. *Just what I'd love to do. Not!* she thought.

Shona flicked her long blond hair over her shoulder and turned to another girl. "Hi, Jane! You'll never guess what I'm having—"

"As if we care!" whispered a disgusted voice at Molly's side as Shona and the other girl walked away together.

Molly turned and grinned at her best friend. "Hi, Narinder."

Narinder Kumar had an oval face and big dark eyes. Her shiny black braids reached down to her waist and her eyebrows were drawn together in a frown. "Sorry, but I can't stand Shona Lamb. She's so spoiled!"

"She can be a little annoying," Molly agreed. "But I don't mind her. Listen, there's the bell."

In the classroom, Molly opened her backpack so Flame could jump out. He gave himself a shake and then began washing. Molly knew that Flame was only visible to her, but she couldn't help looking around nervously. When no one seemed to notice Flame, though, she relaxed.

The teacher took attendance. Everyone answered as their names were called. ". . . Molly Paget," called Miss Garret.

There was no reply.

"Molly?" Miss Garret said again.

Narinder nudged Molly. "Miss Garret's calling your name."

Molly did a double take. She had been watching Flame leap from desk to desk, his bushy white tail streaming out behind him. "Sorry! Here, Miss Garret!" she shouted.

"Thank you, Molly," Miss Garret said patiently. She finished the attendance list and put it away before speaking to the class. "Now, everyone, we won't be

doing any schoolwork today. We're all
going to watch the younger children
perform their Christmas play in an
hour, so we've got just enough time for
a quick clean up."

When Molly, Narinder, and everyone
else groaned Miss Garret smiled.

"Cheer up! It won't take long. Abi

and Heather, would you organize the bookshelves . . ." She began giving out jobs to the class, ". . . And Molly and Narinder, perhaps you could clean up the art stuff, please?"

"Okay, Miss Garret!" Molly jumped up helpfully.

She and Narinder arranged the paper, paints, and brushes. Molly spotted a big

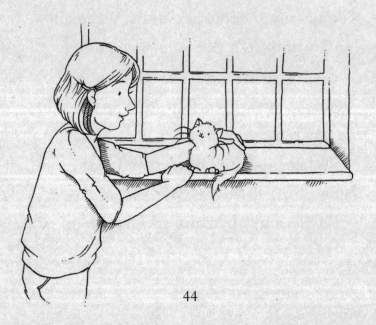

spray can of fake snow on a high shelf.
"Hey, look at this. I've got a great idea."

"What are you going to do?"
Narinder asked.

"Wait and see!" Molly slipped the can
under her school outfit.

While Narinder was putting the last
few things away, Molly wandered across
to the window where Flame was
curled up.

"What is that? Is it something nice to
eat?" the tiny kitten meowed eagerly.

"No, it's fake snow," Molly whispered.
"I'm going to spray snowflakes on the
window as a surprise for everyone."

Flame blinked at her. "What is
snow?"

Molly looked at him in surprise—

maybe it didn't snow where Flame came from. "It has to get very cold and then rain freezes in pretty patterns and white snowflakes float down from the sky. It's so beautiful," she explained. "I'm really hoping for a white Christmas."

Flame's emerald eyes widened in astonishment. "Snow comes from the sky? I would like to see it very much."

"I'll show you what it looks like!" Molly held the can up to the window and gently pressed the button. Nothing happened, so she shook the can hard and then tried again. Just then, someone tapped her on the shoulder.

"Molly, have you—" Shona began.

Molly lifted her finger as she turned

around, but a blast of white foam shot out with a loud whooshing sound. "Oh, no! The button's stuck!" she gasped, trying to free the nozzle.

Shona gave a loud shriek as a powerful jet of fake snow shot all over her clothes.

Chapter
FOUR

Molly finally managed to stop the can
from spraying. She stared at Shona in
horror.

A thick layer of fake snow covered
her from her neck to her waist. It was
dripping off the ends of her long blond
hair and splatting onto the floor in
soggy white blobs.

"Um, sorry . . ." Molly said lamely.

"I can't believe what you've done!"
Shona howled. "Look at my hair! It's
ruined!"

There were muffled giggles from Narinder and some other girls, but Molly didn't laugh. She felt terrible.

Miss Garret hurried over and began mopping up the sticky mess with handfuls of paper towels. "Calm down, Shona, this stuff washes out." She turned to Molly. "Why were you messing around with that spray can?"

"I was going to make snowflakes on the windows, but the nozzle got stuck," Molly explained.

"Oo-oh, you liar!" Shona burst out. "She did it on purpose, Miss Garret! She aimed right at me and made a big long squirt! She's just jealous because I have new boots *and* I'm getting a pony for Christmas!"

Molly blinked at Shona in disbelief. "I couldn't care less about your lousy boots and your stupid old pony!"

"That's enough, both of you!" Miss Garret said, frowning. "I'll speak to you about this later, Molly. Come to the bathroom, Shona. We're going to have to wash your hair and clothes. The rest of you had better go into the hall. The play's about to begin."

Molly hung back as Miss Garret and Shona and most of her classmates filed out. "Can I help it if the spray can decides to malfunction?" she said to Flame.

"It was very bad luck," Flame meowed sympathetically. "I am sorry that I could not use my magic to help you."

"That's okay. I know you couldn't give yourself away," Molly said.

Narinder ran up, grinning widely. "That was *so* hilarious! Serves that snobby Shona right. Stick to your story about spraying her accidentally and you'll be okay!"

"But it really was an accident," Molly protested.

"Yeah, right!" Narinder said. "I'm going to the bathroom. See you in the hall."

"But . . ." Molly gave up. "Come on, Flame," she whispered, shrugging. "I bet you've never seen a school play." As she went into the hallway, Flame scampered along at her heels.

Molly almost bumped into two older girls who were waiting just outside the classroom. She recognized them as Alice and Jane, two girls from the class above hers. They both lived near Shona and often hung out with her.

Alice was tall and thin and Jane was smaller with glasses.

As Molly went to walk past, Alice stuck out a skinny leg, so Molly almost tripped. "Oops. Sorry. It was an accident," she sneered.

"Yeah! Like what you did to Shona," Jane piped up, glaring at Molly through her glasses. "You'd better watch your back."

"Whatever!" Molly said, shrugging, but her heart beat fast as she walked quickly away from the bigger girls.

Molly tried to enjoy the school play. The younger kids were really cute in their angel wings and tinsel halos, but Alice and Jane's threat was still on her mind.

The rest of the day seemed to drag and Molly only managed to eat a tiny bit of her lunch, even though it was turkey with all the trimmings. The moment the school bell rang, Molly headed for the coatroom.

"Come on, Flame, can you quickly jump into my bag again? We don't want to bump into those two mean girls!" she urged.

She said a hurried good-bye to

Narinder at the gate. "Sorry I'm in such a rush. I've . . . er . . . got to hurry home today," she stuttered. "I'll call you!"

Narinder looked surprised. "Okay. See you!" she said, waving.

To Molly's relief, the bus was waiting at the bus stop. She managed to jump onto it, just before it pulled away. She got home safely and was hanging her

backpack in the hall when her mom appeared from upstairs.

"Hello, love. You look upset. Is something wrong?" Mrs. Paget asked.

"I . . . um, had a little accident," Molly began. She told her about spraying Shona. "And everyone thinks I did it on purpose!"

"But of course you didn't!" Mrs. Paget said indignantly. "You sometimes act without thinking first, but you don't have a mean bone in your body!" She gave Molly a hug. "Don't worry about it. It'll all be forgotten about by next semester."

"Do you think so?" Molly asked, biting her lip.

"Definitely," Mrs. Paget said firmly.

She turned toward the plain white Christmas cake on the kitchen table. Icing pens, food coloring, and icing lay next to it. "How would you like to decorate the cake for me? I was about to start it, but I really need to run out to the store."

"Cool!" Molly said, immediately cheering up. "Just leave it to me, Mom!"

As soon as she'd waved good-bye to her mom, Molly came back into the kitchen and began making a robin out of icing. Flame sat on a kitchen chair, watching in fascination as she put the robin on the cake and then made squiggly lines with the icing pens.

Molly looked down at her work so

far. "Not bad. But it needs something else," she said, frowning. "I know! I'll make a snowman. I wonder if Mom's got any of that white ready-made icing stuff left."

Climbing onto a kitchen chair, she peered into the cabinet above the table. She stood up on her tiptoes and poked around behind a stack of cans. "I can't see any—"

"Look out!" Flame meowed warningly as Molly's elbow brushed against the cans.

It was too late. Three heavy cans fell out and landed right on the cake. *Thud!* The cake broke apart and icing and pieces of cake shot all over the table.

"Oh, no!" Molly groaned in dismay.

Flame stood up on his back legs
and rested his front paws on the table.
"Do not worry, Molly. I will help you,"
he purred.

Molly felt a warm tingling down her

spine as bright sparks ignited in Flame's silky white fur and his whiskers crackled with electricity. He lifted a tiny glittering white paw and sent a laser beam of silver sparks toward the ruined cake.

As Molly watched, the sparkling beam moved back and forth, forming the cake back into shape from the bottom up. "Wow! It's just like watching special effects in a sci-fi movie!" she said delightedly.

The cake was half-fixed again, when Flame's sparkling ears twitched. "Someone is coming!" he warned.

A second later, Molly heard the front door slam and voices echoed in the hall. "Hello, is anyone here? Surprise,

surprise!" called Gran Paget.

"Oh, no!" Molly gasped in panic, jumping down from the chair. "What's she doing here? Do something, Flame!"

Chapter
FIVE

Flame's whiskers crackled with another bright burst of power.

As Molly watched, everything went into fast forward. The laser beam whizzed back and forth, reforming the cake in triple-quick time. *Whump!* The cake plonked itself on the plate. *Whoosh!* The cans zoomed into the air. One, two, three—they stacked themselves in the cabinet. *Slam!* The cabinet door closed.

Just as the last fizzing spark faded

from Flame's white fur, Gran Paget
came into the kitchen. Gramps and
Molly's dad were with her.

"Gran! Gramps!" Molly cried, hugging
both of them.

"Hello, honey," Gramps said, kissing her cheek. "I bet you weren't expecting us, were you? We wanted to come a few days early to do some shopping and sightseeing. Your dad just picked us up from the train station."

"I wanted it to be a surprise. I don't know how I managed to keep it a secret," Mr. Paget said, grinning at his daughter.

A small flicker of unease rose in Molly's mind. "Er. . . Dad? Does Mom know about this?" she whispered to him.

"Not yet. But she's going to be delighted. I can't wait to see the look on her face!" he replied.

Neither can I, Molly thought,

remembering the state the spare room was in.

She heard the front door slam. "I'm back," called Mrs. Paget.

"Uh-oh," Molly breathed, running out to meet her mom and almost colliding with her. "Guess who's here! Gran and Gramps!"

Mrs. Paget almost jumped out of her skin. She dropped one of her bags and groceries began rolling everywhere. "Molly! Do you have to dart about like that?" she scolded.

"Oops, sorry!" Molly apologized, picking up the groceries.

Her dad and grandparents came out of the kitchen to help and soon everyone was laughing. Mrs. Paget hugged the grandparents. "What a lovely surprise," she said, looking hard at her husband.

"Time for a cup of tea and a muffin!" Mr. Paget said hurriedly.

"I'll fill the teapot," Molly said, rushing back into the kitchen.

Her mom followed her in. As she caught sight of the Christmas cake, she stopped dead. "Molly? Are you responsible for this?" she exclaimed.

"Um . . . yes. Sorry it didn't turn out very well . . ." Molly said over her shoulder. She was so grateful that Flame had put the cake back together in the nick of time that she had completely forgotten about the lopsided robin and messy squiggles of icing.

"But it's wonderful!" her mom said. "What a lovely snow scene, with a robin on a fence, and I love the snow kitten."

Snow kitten? Molly spun round.

A big grin broke out on her face as she saw that the cake was even better than before the cans had fallen on it. She bent down to look under the table where Flame was sitting. "Thanks, Flame," she whispered.

Flame winked at her and began purring loudly. Suddenly he gave a startled cry as a pair of arms shot under the table and grabbed him.

"How did that cat get in?" Gran scolded. "You're going outside, right now! Animals have no place in kitchens!" Before Molly could react, she opened the back door, threw Flame outside, and shut the door firmly.

Molly stared at her. "But it's cold out there! And Flame's only a tiny kitten!" she protested.

"He'll be fine. He's got a nice thick fur coat to keep him warm," Gran said, dusting off her hands.

Molly scowled. She marched across and opened the back door. "Flame's

my kitten. If he has to stay outside,
I'm staying with him!" she said
stubbornly.

"Now, Molly. Don't be rude . . ." her
mom warned gently.

"I don't care what anyone says!"
Molly fumed. "I'll stay out here all
night if I have to!" She picked Flame
up and cradled him against her. She
could feel him trembling. "Flame lives
in the house. Tell her, Mom."

"Calm down, Molly. I think your
gran thought Flame was just a stray
who'd gotten in somehow. She didn't
know you had a new kitten and I
don't suppose your dad thought to tell
her," Mrs. Paget said reasonably. She
turned to Gran. "Molly's right. Flame

does live in the house. He's a very clean kitten."

Gran straightened up her shoulders. She didn't look pleased. "Have it your way then, but I'm afraid I don't agree with spoiling pets. They have to learn their place."

Yes, and Flame's place is with me, Molly thought. She stormed out of the kitchen and hurried up to her bedroom with Flame.

She curled up on her bed and lay there cuddling Flame and feeling miserable. Gran hated Flame. It was unbelievable. How could anyone not love her gorgeous kitten as much as she did?

"It's not fair!" she complained, petting

Flame's fluffy white fur. "Now you'll have to be shut in my bedroom all the time Gran's here."

Flame's bright eyes sparkled with mischief. "I do not think so! Remember how I came to school with you. No one knew that I was there, did they?"

A slow, delighted grin spread across Molly's face. Of course, Flame could make himself invisible whenever he wanted to!

Molly awoke early the next morning and turned over to pet Flame, who was curled up beside her. *Strange,* she thought, *something seems different.*

"Listen? Can you hear anything?" she said to him.

Flame lifted his head and yawned sleepily. "I cannot hear anything."

"Exactly!" Molly cried. She jumped out of bed, threw open the curtains, and peered out of the window. "Oh! It looks so beautiful," she gasped.

The garden looked as if someone had thrown a thick white blanket over all of it. Snow had made bushes and flower beds into soft blurry humps.

Everything gleamed brightly under a clear silver sky.

"Hooray!" Molly did a little dance of happiness. "It *is* going to be a white Christmas this year! Flame! Come and look. It's been snowing all night."

Flame bounded across to the windowsill in a single leap. He stared out at the garden with shining eyes. "Snow is very beautiful," he purred happily, his warm kitten breath fogging the glass.

"Come on, Flame. I'm going to ask Mom and Dad if we can go sledding in the park!" Molly decided, already searching for a warm sweater and old boots.

She found her dad in the living room, finishing his breakfast cup of tea.

"Sledding in the park's a great idea," he said when Molly had finished speaking. "I'd rather come with you, but your Mom and I already promised to take Gran and Gramps for a walk around the big stores."

"Poor you!" Molly said, grinning at the look on his face. "Never mind, we can go sledding another day."

She was about to go out, when some new knitted cushions caught her eye. One had lime green and purple stripes and the other had orange and blue checks. "Wow! Where did those come from?" she asked.

"They were a present from your

gran. She's crazy about knitting," her dad said wryly. "They look . . . um . . . interesting with our red sofa, don't they?"

"Well, you can't miss them!" Molly burst with laughter. "I think I'll call Narinder and ask her if she wants to meet Flame and me at the park," she decided when she could speak again. "Have a nice time shopping, Dad."

"I'll try to," he said mournfully. "See you later. Come back home by lunchtime, sweetie."

"Okay," Molly answered, skipping into the hall.

Ten minutes later, she was bundled up in a warm coat, scarf, and gloves. "Come on, Flame. Let's go and meet 'Rinder," she said, opening the front door.

Flame leaped straight out and then gave a meow of surprise as he sank into the snow. He ran around, jumping sideways, and then he stopped to sniff at the snow. "It tastes delicious," he purred happily, nibbling at it.

Molly laughed as she watched him. Sometimes it was hard to remember that this cute playful kitten was a majestic lion prince. "It might be best if you ride on the sled," she decided.

"We'll get there faster and your feet
will stay warm."

"My magic will keep me warm,"
Flame meowed, but he sprang onto
the boat-shaped, red plastic sled like
Molly suggested and settled down.

Molly set off, dragging her sled and
Flame behind her.

The park was only a couple of
minutes away. Lots of kids were
already there. Some had sleds and others
sat on garbage can lids or plastic bags as
they slid down the snowy slopes. Molly
saw Narinder waving as she came
toward her. "Hi! Isn't this awesome!"
she cried.

"Yeah! I love snow!" Molly said.

"Hey, I didn't know you had a kitten.

Isn't he gorgeous! Where did you get him from?" Narinder said, bending down to pet Flame's fuzzy little head.

Flame purred and rubbed against Narinder's gloved hand.

"I haven't had him long," Molly said quickly, hoping to avoid awkward questions. "Come on. Let's go sledding!"

She and Narinder trudged up the steep snowy slope with their sleds. At the top, Molly sat down and Flame jumped into her lap.

"I'll race you!" Molly said to Narinder.

"You're on!" Narinder shouted back. "Ready? One. Two. Three!"

"Hold on, Flame! Here we go!" Molly cried, pushing off with her hands.

Molly and Narinder flew down the slope, side by side. Flame's silky white fur blew back in the cold air.

"Whe-ee-e!" Molly yelled, grinning across at Narinder as her sled edged forward. "We're winning!"

Suddenly, near the bottom of the slope, she felt the sled skidding sideways. The front of it clipped a small bank of snow and it spun around and tipped over. Molly shot into the air and landed in the soft powdery snow with Flame still on her lap.

Narinder whizzed past, yelling triumphantly.

"Next time!" Molly shouted. Giggling, she started to get up. "Wasn't that awesome, Flame—"

"Well if it isn't that snob who sprayed stuff all over me in class!" said a voice. Shona Lamb stood there with her hands on her hips. She wore a pretty pink ski jacket and fluffy earmuffs. "Listen to her talking to her kitten. As if it's going to answer her!"

Molly's tummy felt queasy as she saw that Shona wasn't alone. Alice and Jane, Shona's mean older friends were with her.

Chapter
SIX

"Now you're in for it!" warned
Shona, scooping up a big snowball.

"Yeah!" Jane said, bending down and
making a snowball, too.

"Three against one isn't fair!" Molly
said in a wobbly voice as she got to
her feet. She quickly placed Flame on
the sled out of harm's way. He
stood there, tiny legs planted wide,
his fur and bushy tail bristling with
fury.

"Tough!" Alice said, grinning nastily.

Molly's mouth dried. Flame might
want to help her, but he couldn't use
his magic without giving himself away.
Narinder was at the bottom of the
long slope.

She was on her own.

A snowball hit Molly on the arm, but
the powdery snow broke and it didn't
really hurt. Another one landed on her

back and then one hit her ear with a stinging blow. Molly hardly had time to make a snowball of her own and throw it, before she was hit again.

"Ow!" she cried as another snowball hit her neck and icy snow trickled inside her coat collar. "That's enough. You've paid me back," she said, trying not to cry.

"Maybe she's right," Shona said uncertainly. "Let's go."

"No, wait! I haven't finished with her yet!" Jane had a mean look on her face. She was patting her gloved hands together, making a snowball into a firm lump. Before Molly realized what she was going to do, Jane drew back her arm and aimed at Flame.

"No!" Molly screamed, throwing herself in front of him. The hard snowball smacked into her cheek with bruising force.

Molly gasped, stunned. Her cheek felt as if it was on fire and she felt sick and dizzy.

"Now you've really hurt her!" Shona said worriedly. "She's all white and shaky!"

Jane and Alice exchanged glances. "Run!" Jane said.

Shona came over to Molly. "Are you all right? I'm sorry. I didn't mean for it to go so far," she said, biting her lip.

"Just leave me alone," Molly murmured shakily.

As Shona ran after her friends, Molly's

legs gave way and she sank onto the
snow. Flame scampered up to her in an
instant. "Quick, Molly. Put me inside
your coat," he meowed urgently.

Molly did so. As soon as Flame was
hidden from sight, Molly heard a faint
crackling as sparks ignited in his fur,
and there was a soft glow from inside
her coat as Flame's whiskers fizzed with

power. The familiar warm tingling
spread down her back and Molly felt a
gentle prickling in her sore cheek. The
pain drained away, just as if she had
poured it down the sink.

"That's much better. Thanks, Flame,"
she whispered.

Flame touched her chin with his tiny
cold nose. "You saved me from being
hurt, Molly. You were very brave."

Molly's heart swelled with a surge of
affection for him. "I'm not really. I just
couldn't bear to think of anything
happening to you. I love having you
as my friend. I hope you can stay with
me forever."

"I will stay for as long as I can,"
Flame purred gently.

"Molly! Are you all right?" Narinder's breath puffed out in the cold air as she came panting up the slope. "I feel awful. I saw those bullies coming at you, but I couldn't get to you quickly enough to help."

Molly grinned. "Don't worry about it, 'Rinder, it's hard to run uphill in the snow. Anyway, I'm okay. And I think they'll leave me alone now that they've gotten me back. Come on, let's go back up. I'm definitely going to beat you to the bottom this time!"

"Hi, we're home!" Molly sang out as she dumped her coat and boots and went toward the living room.

Her mom poked her head around the

door. "Shh. Can you be quiet, sweetie? Gran's sleeping in there. We went on a long hunt for some special knitting wool and she's worn out. Did you have a good time in the park?"

"Great, thanks. Where's Dad and Gramps?" Molly asked.

"In the garage, messing around," her mom replied. "They need a little relief after all those stores! Lunch will be ready soon, so don't go far. It's home-made tomato soup."

"Sounds good." Molly went quietly into the living room and sat on the sofa to read a magazine. "There's no need to become invisible, Flame. Gran's asleep. Listen!" she whispered, giggling.

Soft snores rose from the corner chair, where Gran was asleep with her knitting bag in her lap. As Molly watched, the bag slowly tipped forward and a ball of blue wool fell out and rolled across the carpet.

Flame couldn't resist. He gave a tiny eager meow and pounced on it. Play-growling and lashing his tail, he chased the ball of wool around the back of Gran's chair.

Molly bit back a burst of laughter as Flame reappeared with the ball of wool held proudly in his mouth. He tossed his head and the ball of wool tightened. Gran's knitting seemed to jump out of the bag. On the end of the ball of wool there was a half-finished, blue and white striped sock.

"Uh-oh. Now you've really done it!" Molly breathed. She crept forward to rescue the knitting. But it was too late.

Gran opened her eyes, yawned, and sat up. As she spotted Flame she gave a gasp of horror. "My knitting! You little menace! What have you done? Just wait

until I get my hands on you!"

Flame laid his ears back and yowled with panic. He tried to run away, but the wool was wound tightly around his legs, and he fell over his own feet.

Red-faced, Gran got up from the chair but Molly was already bounding across the room. She got to Flame first. "Stop moving," she scolded gently, untangling him as quickly as she could. "That's it! You'd better scoot! Gran's on the warpath!"

Flame didn't need telling twice. Flattening his ears, he zoomed out and ran upstairs. Molly picked up the mess of wool and knitting and handed it to Gran.

Gran had a face like thunder. "That

sock's ruined and I don't like the idea of using the wool again after that little beggar's been chewing it. Those socks were for your dad. I'll never have them finished for Christmas now. I told you that kitten would be nothing but trouble!"

"Sorry, Gran," Molly said in a subdued voice. *Why didn't Gran just buy socks, like normal people did, anyway?* she thought. "Flame didn't mean to be naughty. He was just playing."

"Soup's ready! Molly could you go and tell your dad and Gramps, please?" Mrs. Paget called from the hall.

"Will do, Mom. Phew!" Molly breathed gratefully, escaping as quickly as she could.

SEVEN

Molly had Flame in her bag as she walked out to the car with her dad the following afternoon. It was the day before Christmas Eve and they were all going shopping at the Christmas market in the square.

"I've been meaning to say thank you to you and Flame," her dad said.

"What for?" Molly asked, puzzled.

"For saving me from having to wear blue and white striped socks!" he said, smiling.

Molly laughed and gave him a friendly shove, and then her face grew serious. "Gran was furious about having her knitting ruined. I don't think she'll ever like Flame now," she said sadly.

"Oh, you never know. Gran's bark is worse than her bite," her dad said.

"Really?" Molly said. Then, seeing her grandparents coming out of the house, she quickly got into the car with Flame.

As her dad drove them all into town, Molly counted out her money. She had been saving it up for weeks and had enough to buy gifts for everyone— including Flame. It was exciting to think of all the lovely things she was going to buy.

The market was crowded and colorful. It was full of exciting stands, selling things from all around the world. Colored lightbulbs flashed on the huge Christmas tree and tinsel glittered under the streetlights. People wrapped in hats and scarves walked around carrying bags and lots of presents.

As Molly, her parents, and her grandparents strolled among the stands Flame popped his head out of her bag. His nose twitched as he enjoyed the smells of roasting chestnuts and hot spiced chocolate.

"Isn't this great?" Molly whispered to Flame, looking at some pretty silk scarves. "I'm going to buy one of these for Mom."

Flame didn't answer, but Molly was too busy to notice. She paused to listen to some carol singers holding lanterns, their sweet voices rising on the frosty air. At other stands, she bought lavender bags for Gran, a key ring for Gramps, and a new wallet for her dad.

"I'm doing really well with buying presents," she said, glancing down at Flame. But his head wasn't sticking up out of her bag. "Flame? Are you taking a nap?" She reached her hand inside the bag to pet him and her fingers brushed against a tightly curled up trembling little body. "What's wrong?" she asked in concern.

"My uncle's spies are here. I can sense them," Flame said softly. "I must hide!"

Molly's heart clenched with panic. Flame was in terrible danger. Her mind raced as she tried to decide what to do. There was no way she was letting anyone hurt Flame!

Suddenly she had an idea. "Don't

worry! We're leaving," she whispered to Flame.

Spotting her parents at a nearby cheese stand, Molly ran straight over. "Can we go home?" she pleaded. "I feel awful. I think I'm going to be sick!"

Gran and Gramps appeared, holding some bags. "What's wrong?" asked Gramps.

"It's Molly. She feels sick," Mr. Paget answered.

"It's probably all the free samples she's tried," Gran said. "I think she'll be okay in a minute."

"No, I won't!" Molly insisted. She felt desperate. Rolling her eyes, she gave a loud groan and clutched her tummy. "I think I'm dying! It'll be all your fault if I collapse right here in the market."

Even Gran looked alarmed.

"Don't be so dramatic, Molly. It's only a little tummy ache," her dad said mildly, but he looked worried. "Perhaps we'd better take you home."

"We're almost finished shopping, aren't we? Let's all go back," Gramps said.

Molly could have kissed him. She flashed him a grateful smile and then remembered that she was supposed to be feeling sick.

As they all hurried toward the parking lot, she pet Flame's trembling little body. "Hang on! We'll be out of here soon," she whispered.

Molly didn't see the dark shadowy shapes slipping between the stands or the narrow cruel eyes that searched the crowded market.

"He is very close," growled a cold voice.

"Ebony will reward us well for finding the young prince," hissed the other spy.

"I'm being allowed to stay up late tonight. We're all going to midnight Mass at the church. You'll love it!" Molly said happily the following afternoon.

Flame was curled up on her blanket, surrounded by pieces of shiny wrapping paper, ribbons, and tape. He was back

to his normal self, now that the danger from his uncle's spies seemed to be far behind him.

Molly was wrapping her presents in shiny wrapping paper. "I hope those horrible mean cats keep on going until they jump into the sea and sink! And then you can stay with me forever," she said to Flame.

Flame blinked up at her. "They may come back and then I will have to leave at once. Do you understand, Molly?" he meowed seriously.

"Yes," Molly answered in a small voice. "But I'm not going to think about that."

She finished wrapping her presents and putting bows on them. "I'll go and put them under the tree now," she said to herself.

Leaving Flame napping, she went downstairs into the living room. Gramps was reading a newspaper and Gran was knitting. She had started a new scarf in pink, brown, and yellow stripes.

There was the sound of voices from the kitchen.

"Hi, Gran. Hi, Gramps," Molly said, bending down to put her presents with

the others. A sudden thought struck her.
Surely there was one missing. "Oh, no,"
she gasped. "I've forgotten to buy one
for Flame." In all the rush of getting
Flame away from his enemies, she'd
completely forgotten to get him a
present.

"What's wrong, sweetie?" Gramps
asked, looking up from his paper.

Molly told him. ". . . and Flame's going to be the only one without a present to open on Christmas morning," she finished glumly.

"Oh, that's a shame," Gran said.

Molly looked at her in surprise. It sounded like she really meant it. "I'll just have to go to the store and get one. Maybe Dad will take me. I'll ask him," she said on her way to the door.

"I think it's too late, dear," Gramps said. "The stores all close early on Christmas Eve."

"Oh, yes," Molly remembered with dismay. She stopped and turned back around. This was awful. What was she going to do? Flame would have to go without a present.

Gran looked thoughtful. "I've got an idea," she said, producing the scrap of blue and white sock from her knitting bag. "I think I could make this into a toy mouse."

"Do you mean it?" Molly looked at her gran. Maybe she *did* like Flame a little bit, after all. She flew over and gave her a huge hug. "That would be perfect! Thanks, Gran. You're the best!"

Chapter
EIGHT

Molly felt full of the magic of Christmas as she walked into the church. The ancient walls flickered with the light of countless candles, and footsteps echoed on the stone floor.

Even though it was long past Molly's usual bedtime, she didn't feel tired.

Flame was in her bag. And it didn't matter if everyone could see him. Animals and their owners were all welcome for the special Christmas Eve service.

"Isn't it gorgeous in here?" she

whispered to him, looking at the candlelight flickering on the stained-glass windows and the big vases of flowers, holly, and ivy.

The church was packed and everyone

was in a good mood. There were hot drinks, muffins, and bags of fruit and nuts to snack on. A special band with amazing instruments from all around the world played and dancers performed folk dances. And then the church choir sang and everyone joined in with the carols.

Molly caught sight of Shona with her parents. She hesitated for a moment and then waved at her. Shona looked surprised and then she waved back, smiling. "Merry Christmas!" she called.

"Merry Christmas!" Molly replied happily.

"I got my pony. You'll have to come over and see him. He's gorgeous," Shona said.

Molly bit back a grin. She was glad they were friends again, but Shona would never change.

After the service ended, Molly and Flame, her parents, and grandparents all trudged home through the snow. A big silver moon shed its light onto the glittering snow crystals on the ground.

Molly held her bag close to her chest, so that she could pet Flame without anyone noticing. "This has to be the best Christmas Eve ever," she whispered to him.

Just before she went up to bed, Gran put a tiny package into her hand. "For Flame. I hope he likes it," she said.

Molly threw her arms around her and kissed her cheek. "I love you, Gran."

Gran's eyes looked moist and shiny. "I love you, too, Molly."

Molly slipped Flame's present under the tree before she went up to her bedroom. She felt so excited that she was sure she wouldn't sleep a wink. She'd just lie there in the dark, waiting for Christmas day.

After undressing and brushing her teeth, Molly slipped into bed. "Good night, Flame," she whispered, breathing in his sweet kitten smell as she cuddled with him.

Seconds later, she was asleep.

It felt like about five minutes later, when Molly opened her eyes. She was amazed to find the winter light pushing through her curtains.

"Come on, Flame. It's Christmas morning!" She leaped out of bed, threw her dressing gown on over her pajamas, and pushed her feet into her slippers.

She ran down the stairs two at a time, with Flame running at her heels.

"Merry Christmas!" she said, bouncing into the living room.

Her mom and dad and grandparents were already dressed and sitting with hot drinks. They looked up and smiled as Molly burst in.

"Merry Christmas, sweetie," said her dad, pouring more coffee.

"Merry Christmas," chorused her mom and Gran and Gramps.

"Can we open our presents now?" Molly said, going to sit cross-legged on the rug with Flame in her lap.

"We thought you'd never ask!" Gramps said. "We've all been waiting for you to wake up."

Molly unwrapped her presents eagerly. She had some books and music and lots of other cool stuff. But best of all were the new boots she'd been hoping for. "Cool! Thanks so much for my lovely presents, everyone!" she said, putting the boots on right away.

"Interesting look with those pajamas!" her dad joked.

Everyone laughed.

"Here's your present, Flame!" Molly loosened the wrapping paper.

He ripped it open with his sharp teeth and claws, a look of delight on his tiny face. The moment Flame saw Gran's knitted mouse, he gave an excited little meow. Grabbing it in his mouth he padded proudly around the room, his bushy tail high in the air.

"I'm glad someone likes my knitting!" Gran said, giving Molly's dad one of her looks.

Mr. Paget kissed Gran's cheek and then winked at Molly.

Molly choked back a laugh. "Flame adores his mouse, Gran! Um . . . is it okay if I call Narinder and ask if she wants to come and listen to my new CDs later on?" she asked.

"Of course it is," said her mom. "And

then can you hurry up and get dressed? Breakfast's almost ready. It's your favorite."

"Okay," Molly said, going out into the hall.

Suddenly, Flame streaked past her and raced upstairs so fast that he was a tiny white blur. Molly frowned. He'd never done that before.

"Flame? What—" she broke off as a horrible suspicion arose in her mind. She started running after him, her phone call forgotten for the moment.

As Molly reached the landing, there was a bright flash from her open bedroom door. She dashed into her room. Flame stood there, no longer a tiny kitten, but a magnificent young

white lion with a coat that glittered and
glinted with a thousand sparkles. An
older gray lion with a wise and gentle
face stood next to him.

"Prince Flame! We must leave now!" the gray lion growled urgently.

Molly caught her breath as she understood that Flame's enemies had found him again. This time he was going to leave for good.

Flame's emerald eyes crinkled in a fond smile. "Merry Christmas, Molly. Be well, be strong," he rumbled in a velvety growl as a whoosh of silver sparks spun around him. And then he and the old lion disappeared.

"Good-bye, Flame. Take care. I'll never forget you. I hope you regain your throne," Molly said, her heart aching.

Molly knew that she'd remember this Christmas forever. Having Flame as her friend, even for only a short time, was the best present she would ever have. She stood there for a moment longer as she brushed away a tear.

And then she remembered Narinder. As Molly went downstairs to phone her, she found herself smiling.